THE LITTLE POLITICIAN

Martin Wagner is a writer and film-maker living in London. His science-fiction novel *Rachel's Machine* was published by Pinter & Martin in the UK and Mondadori in Italy. His films include the award-winning short film *Summer* and the documentary *Klaus Maria Brandauer: Speer in London*. In 2003 he published the acclaimed *The Little Driver*.

THE LITTLE
POLITICIAN

MARTIN **WAGNER**

A PINTER & MARTIN original paperback

The Little Politician

First published in Great Britain by Pinter & Martin Ltd 2005

ISBN 0-9530964-9-1

British Library Cataloguing-in-Publication Data
A catalogue record for this book is available from the British Library

Set in Garamond

Printed and bound in Great Britain by
Creative Print & Design, Ebbw Vale, Wales

Pinter & Martin Ltd
6 Effra Parade
London SW2 1PS

www.pinterandmartin.com

FOR MARCSI

Joe was the first to know that when your wildest
dreams come true you had better keep an eye on
your feet to see whether they're still touching the
ground. But, what with the election yesterday, the
long night waiting for the results and then he had
had a little too much hot chocolate to celebrate – he
had been so busy that he barely had time to look.
Now they, his feet, were firmly planted on a stack of
telephone books that had been assembled in a hurry
by some men in strange wigs. While over the past few
days the general public had quickly become used to
the fact that Britain would elect its youngest ever
prime minister, few of the people who were meant to
take care of practicalities seemed to have taken
account, that, at the age of nine, Joe would be
considerably shorter than his predecessors.

Prime minister's question time had started and Joe
was meant to pay attention. After all, that was him.
This was the first time Joe had been in parliament,
and the first thing he had noticed was that it was
much smaller than it looked on TV. It seemed odd
being placed opposite the other parties and he
almost felt obliged to disagree with whatever they
had to say.

The first handful of questions were easy enough to
answer – especially the one about what Joe was
planning to do today – but before he knew it, the
leader of the opposition was up on his feet, his smile

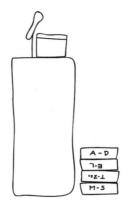

A STACK OF TELEPHONE BOOKS HAD BEEN ASSEMBLED
IN A HURRY BY SOME MEN IN STRANGE WIGS

even less sincere than it had been during the election campaign. Joe was always very wary of sentences containing double negatives, and he was sure the leader of the opposition had said something like 'would or wouldn't you agree that the country shouldn't ...' which sounded suspiciously like a trick question – a bit like 'Have you or haven't you not done your homework?'

'Excuse me,' Joe climbed back up to the despatch box. 'Could you repeat that in plain English?'

This got him his first laugh of his parliamentary career, but only from the benches behind him. How could a thing be funny on one side and not on the other, Joe wondered, even though on this occasion he didn't think he had said anything particularly funny at all.

The leader of the opposition looked a little flustered and seemed to have decided not to pursue the matter any further, whatever it was. Joe wanted to ask *him* a few complicated questions in return, especially about the house which until last night he'd been living in. For example, had he or had he not hidden the remote control from his flat in 10 Downing Street? True, Joe had lots of people to turn on TVs for him now, but they never seemed to choose anything he wanted to watch.

The old man opposite sat down again. There was none of the spring in his step that Joe had noticed during the campaign. Joe almost felt sorry for him. Not only had he lost his job, but he had also been kicked out of his home. Joe wondered whether he and his wife had started packing when the first disastrous exit poll results came in, or if they had really waited until three in the morning. In that case they could be forgiven for not leaving a note saying where everything was.

For the rest of prime minister's questions, Joe simply had to read out the prepared answers he'd been given, which seemed simple enough, apart from when he read out the wrong answer to the wrong question. But no one seemed to notice and before Joe had time to worry about more double negatives from the opposition, the mood changed once again. Another man in a wig announced the next item on the agenda, but apparently this was something Joe was not to be part of for he was suddenly whisked out through the small door and away along quiet corridors as quickly as he had arrived there.

2

'Not bad at all,' whispered Charlie as they proceeded to take several unexpected turns through the Houses of Westminster, as if to shake off some unwanted pursuers. Joe found it hard to keep up with Charlie and though she glanced at him impatiently, she stopped short of pulling him by the hand. Charlie had been Joe's campaign manager and now was his policy adviser, secretary and new best friend all rolled into one. 'I'm so glad you didn't get out your list.'

The list! He checked his back pocket for the list he had written out. Joe had had big plans for the big day, but Charlie had thought it best to take things slowly. First people had to get used to the fact that a nine-year-old was calling the shots – but, after all, who better to run a country than a boy with an open mind and unlimited supplies of energy?

To make the list look prime ministerial, Joe had taken his grandad's old typewriter and spelt his dreams out point by point; one for each of his years, as it turned out.

Things to do when I rule the world:
1. Help the poor
2. Steal from the rich (see 1)
3. No more wars
4. Free chocolate for all

5. All bullies to be locked up
6. Ban all cars *
7. No more borders
8. No more homework
9. Always remember those less fortunate than yourself

'Have you been learning your phrases?' Charlie asked as they approached their destination.

'Sure,' Joe sighed. He hadn't quit school to be subjected to more lists of vocabulary, but he guessed he'd have to do his best if he wanted to be good at his job.

'Help out a mate in trouble?' Charlie prompted him.

'Stand shoulder to shoulder.'

'Good. Peace?'

'A war is simply not on the agenda at this time.'

'War?'

'A war is simply not on the agenda at this time.'

'I can't be asked to do anything today?'

'Timetable for action?'

'Bullies?'

'... whips?' Joe had heard about whips, who made sure that the whole party agreed with each other, but they sounded suspiciously like Stan, who was always after his pocket money.

* Joe used to love cars, like any self-respecting young boy would. But ever since he had been in charge of a shiny red sports car for a day when he was eight, he had changed his mind. But that's another story. *The Little Driver*, Pinter & Martin, 2003.

'Not bad, but these words have to become second nature. Only then will you be a true diplomat.'

Joe wasn't sure he wanted to become a true diplomat. Rather he was hoping to be able to tell people what they *should* hear rather than what they wanted to hear. 'But why can't I just say what I mean?'

'To avoid confusion.'

'But isn't that being dishonest?'

'You can only be dishonest when you say something,' Charlie insisted. 'It's the art of *not* saying anything in the largest possible number of words that makes a truly great politician.'

Joe remembered listening to Churchill's speeches and, as far as he remembered, he always said something worth hearing. 'What about Churchill?' Joe asked, but immediately regretted it.

'Things were different then. Now we don't talk to the public. We talk to the press. Which does have its downsides, but usually it's very beneficial.'

'Why?'

'We save a fortune on postage.'

Joe sighed. He was sure that Charlie didn't talk in this coded language to her friends. It wasn't the first time Joe had envied Charlie. Charlie seemed to be in charge of pretty much everything – including his list – and she didn't even have to go through the bother of getting elected.

They were approaching an imposing-looking door. 'These people have been paying for your campaign. Be nice to them,' Charlie said. 'But don't make any promises that you intend to keep until you've cleared them with me!' Joe was surprised to see a whiff of cigarette smoke coming from under the door and suddenly he knew he didn't fancy going in there much. Then before Charlie could protest, Joe had slipped off down another corridor which looked far more promising.

3

After going round some corners and up some stairs to make sure Charlie couldn't catch up with him, Joe realised he had ended up in a corridor of MPs' offices. He wondered whether the Houses of Westminster had a right wing and a left wing, but soon realised that MPs from both sides of the house were represented here. The doors of some of the MPs' offices had been left ajar and he tried to peek into their rooms.

Joe knew Charlie would be upset that he was missing his appointment, but he had had enough meetings to last a lifetime. That morning he had already met the Queen, with whom, frankly, he had not much in common. Especially as he, being prime minister, was into democracy and he had never seen her down at the polling station. She was pleasant enough, though, even if she did seem lonely in her big house, spending her spare time doing impersonations of her subjects. He made a mental note to get her to come round to his mum's house for tea to give her some new material.

The second meeting had been even more bizarre. He had been introduced to the Chief of the Defence Staff who proceeded to tell him to imagine the worst – in other words Britain blown to smithereens and little Joe with it. What would he want the captains of his five nuclear subs to do?

Luckily, to make the whole thing easier, Joe was given some sort of multiple-choice answers: wipe out a few of the enemy's cities in retaliation; go and join some other friendly country to help out with whatever needed doing; or let them decide for themselves.

He was given five sheets of paper and envelopes so that he could write out his instructions in longhand. He had pondered what to do in his office for hours before realising that there was only one possible solution.

He put a blank sheet in each envelope and sealed them, hoping that no one would ever open them, and making a mental note to add nuclear disarmament to his list. After all, it had been over 50 years since the last war – or at least since the last one that people talked about as a war. The rest were conflicts, and Joe also made a mental note to look up the difference between these two words in the dictionary as soon as he got a chance.

But maybe there hadn't been wars because he *had* nuclear weapons, Joe wondered. It may be good to have them dismantled secretly. And maybe then, if one of his generals, in the heat of battle, jumped to the conclusion that the solution to the threat of your home being destroyed by a nuclear bomb is to destroy someone else's, he'd come to thank him.

Wouldn't it be funny, Joe wondered, if I tried to disarm the nuclear bomb, then discovered that someone had already done it before me?

4

Most of the MPs' offices were empty and Joe had almost given up on the idea of meeting someone interesting when he came upon a man standing in the middle of an office looking pensive.

'Hi, I'm Joe,' Joe said, always having been taught that it is arrogant to assume people know who you are.

The MP turned to him, embarrassed, and Joe saw that he was holding a golf club. Placed in the corner of the office was an electronic gadget which returned your golf ball on the rare occasion that you actually hit the device.

'I beg your pardon, Prime Minister ... I was just...' The MP's face had turned so red that Joe was beginning to wish he hadn't entered. 'You see, Prime Minister, I don't get many visits. Especially not from the PM.'

'What are you doing?' Joe asked, for something to say, even though it was pretty obvious what he was doing.

'Er ...' the MP stuttered, presumably not having thought that there could be a graceful way out of this situation. 'I'm thinking,' he decided.

'About what?'

'About this lot,' the man pointed to his desk. It consisted of two trays of paperwork. One pile reached halfway up to the ceiling and the other was barely two centimetres high. All things considered, Joe had the sneaking suspicion that the one with the large pile of paper wasn't the out tray.

'My correspondence,' the MP explained. 'This lot came in this morning.'

Joe was astonished. This must mean that yesterday's work was done and dusted. 'You go through all that in a day?' Joe said, more than little impressed. This man deserved a round of golf!

'Er ... I'm afraid not, Prime Minister.' The man put down his golf club and pointed to a door. 'The rest is filed in there.'

Joe turned the door handle.

'No!' the MP shouted, but it was already too late. The door opened and a mountain of paper fell on Joe, who had to struggle in order not to be buried alive. His head popped out from the middle of the mountain of paper. The MP looked at him apologetically.

'These are all letters to be dealt with?' Joe said once he had spat out the paperclips stuck in his mouth. He picked up a letter and glanced at it. *Dear MP, I know how busy you are,* the letter read, *but I've tried everything to get the council to fix my dripping tap ...*

The MP shrugged his shoulders. 'You see, Prime Minister, at election time we are men and women of the people, going from door to door promising everything under the sun. And then, if we have the misfortune to be elected, all this lot comes in.' The MP leant sadly on his golf club. 'I simply don't have time to think,' he added as an afterthought. Joe

JOE'S HEAD POPPED OUT FROM THE MIDDLE OF THE MOUNTAIN OF PAPER

decided that this clearly showed the man up as a liar, but he thought it better not to get into that.

'In my first six months as an MP I tried to get on top of things, but it was impossible. For starters no one tells you how to do your job. I went back to my constituency every Friday, tried to deal with all this lot in person, but the problems got too much for me. My wife left me.' The MP sighed one of the deepest sighs Joe had every heard. 'And even if I wanted to help all these people ... I don't know anything about drains, or legislation ...'

'What?' Joe couldn't believe what he was hearing.

'Once MPs were professionals, good at something. They had real jobs and became MPs because they wanted to give something back to the community. They were good at their professions, manufacturing, farming, the army, whatever. These days all we MPs are good at is at getting elected. Well, not that good overall, but I guess I was one of the lucky ones.' The MP looked at the mountain of paper and sighed. 'Or unlucky ones.'

Joe sat down in the chair and picked up the phone. 'Could we get some hot chocolate in here, please.'

'Hot chocolate?' The MP looked disappointed.

'Pass me the first letter,' Joe said.

The MP put down his golf club with a sigh, and gave Joe a letter from the pile.

Dear MP, it read, *I know how busy you are, but my cat Alan lost his leg when the council tried to recycle his litter tray with him still in it ...*

When Joe next looked up and glanced at the clock on the wall, it was four hours later. The pile in the out tray must have grown by about a centimetre while the in tray now stretched even higher, stopping only a few centimetres short of the ceiling. Joe hadn't counted on the second post and swore to abolish it as soon as he had a chance.

There was a knock at the door and Joe turned. It was Charlie. 'We've been looking for you everywhere. Then I had the bright idea to trace the pots of hot chocolate.' To be honest, Joe was very happy to be found. This hands-on politics sure was exhausting. He was bored with drains and pets and noisy neighbours. He suspected that the MP would get back to his golf as soon as Joe left, but who could blame him?

Out of the corner of his eye, Joe couldn't help but notice an office which was about as tidy as the other one had been untidy. Maybe the golf-playing MP was just stringing him along, and Joe was very happy to see that all that work could be dealt with efficiently, even if it was by an MP of the opposition party. He was curious, and despite Charlie's condescending look, he decided to take a look.

'What's going on here?' Joe asked more in admiration than anything else. The MP was at his computer, busily pressing buttons, and somewhere in the corner a printer was rattling out letters.

'Hi, Joe,' the MP said, a little overfamiliarly, though that didn't really bother Joe. 'Just dealing with my mail.' Instead of an out tray, Joe noticed a postbag stuffed to the rim with sealed envelopes.

'You see, PM, all I have to do is enter my constituent's address on my screen, answer a few simple multiple-choice questions, and it spits out a letter suitable for any occasion.'

Joe looked impressed.

'Give me a problem!' the MP said.

'What?'

'Any problem you want me to deal with.' If he were to be honest, Joe's problem was with understanding this whole politics thing, but surely that would be more than the MP's computer could deal with.

'Can I make one up?'

'Sure.'

'OK.' Joe thought. 'My three-legged cat fell in the drain which should have been fixed by the housing office, and the council is refusing to give me tax relief for the funeral expenses.'

'All right,' the MP said and tapped into his computer. 'Let's see ... 'Cat' ... 'Drain' ... 'Housing office' ... 'Tax' ... ' After what could not have been more than twenty seconds, he leant back in satisfaction, while behind him the printer went into action. 'There is your reply!'

Joe walked over to the printer and removed the sheet. He must admit it did look rather professional. It read:

Dear Miss Joe,
I am very sorry to hear about your cat's
housing problems, but I'm afraid that after
careful consideration we feel that this is a
matter you should raise with Mr Drain
instead.
Please don't hesitate to contact me if you
should have any further comments or
suggestions.
Glad to be of help,
Your MP
PS: If you want to pay less tax, vote for us
next time.

'But this doesn't make sense,' Joe pointed out.

'What?' the MP ripped the sheet of paper from Joe's hand and glanced at it. 'Well, it was a silly problem anyway.'

Joe knew it was silly, but people with silly problems also wanted to be listened to.

'So what if they contacted you again?'

'Hardly anyone ever does. People with problems like that don't have time to write letters. They are either too busy working or can't afford the postage, or both.'

'But what if they do?'

'Now this you *are* going to love. Do it.'

'Do what?'

'Write in.'

Joe was beginning to feel a little silly, but, to be honest, he was also rather curious. 'Dear MP,' he said, 'I'm sorry, but your letter is complete gibberish. Yours faithfully, Joe.'

The MP tapped on his keyboard again. 'There!' The printer spat out another sheet. It read:

Dear Constituent,
Many thanks for taking the time to write in about my previous letter, which you called 'gibberish.' Please accept this letter, which does make sense, as our apology.
As that problem has now been addressed, rest assured that you won't hear from me again.
Yours truly,
Your MP
PS: If you want to pay less tax, vote for us next time.

'See – problem solved! Now, if you'll excuse me, my constituents need me.'

Joe had to admit that this solution was rather elegant, but, as he left the MP hitting the keys of his computer, he thought of the MP practising his putting, unable to face the people who had elected him. Maybe it was in the nature of politics that if you did the job properly, you went insane. Joe wondered why anyone did it. Surely simply getting attention without giving back anything in return wouldn't be reward enough for anyone.

As he rejoined Charlie, who was impatiently pointing at her watch, Joe considered whether it might be true that sometimes the people wc don't hear from are the ones who care the most.

'Where's the fire?' Joe joked as he entered the cabinet room, but the round of gloomy faces told him that things were serious. Even though the meeting couldn't start without him, it was clear that there had already been some heated discussion.

Joe took his place. As he looked around the cabinet table, he realised that his ministers were beginning to look familiar. Like being at a new school, it hadn't taken much time to figure out who were the nice guys and who were the bullies.

Joe was quickly briefed on what had been going on. A country was not behaving as it should and already the cabinet was talking about invasion. But invading countries sounded pretty serious and Joe had always assumed that one shouldn't do it unless it was really really necessary. A bit like homework.

'It's simply a question of human rights!' exclaimed the foreign minister, who Joe had previously identified as not being a bully. 'We have to help liberate it!'

Joe found it hard to suppress a laugh. He had learnt about this country at school. Over a third of the world's oil supply came from there, so it was hardly surprising that people were interested in it. Attacking this country because of human rights abuses was about the same as buying *Power Rangers Magazine* for the articles. He and his friends were only interested in the free toys and the centre spread.

'And I just *know* they have WMDs!' the foreign secretary shouted.

'WMDs?' Joe looked puzzled. He was only halfway through his vocabulary, and W was still a long way off.

'Weapon of mass destruction, Prime Minister.'

'Oh, like our nuclear subs.' Joe knew all about weapons of mass destruction. He had always wanted some, but now that he had plenty he was not so sure any more. 'Does this country pose an actual threat?' Joe asked. He was worried that he wouldn't be able to dismantle his nuclear subs in time.

'Frankly, who doesn't?' the foreign secretary sighed.

'Does Switzerland pose a threat?' Joe asked, but got no reply. The foreign minister turned back to the whole table. 'We should make immediate plans to stabilise this part of the world.'

'By starting a war?' Joe asked.

The minister looked at him, obviously irritated. 'If you want to put it that way.'

'And how are we going to explain that to the public?'

'Well, I think explaining it may be a bad idea. They may not agree. It's better to keep it in terms people can understand.'

'How?'

'They are afraid.'

'Of what?'

'Weapons of mass destruction.'

Joe was beginning to feel as if they were going round in circles here. He was tired and hadn't been sleeping well ever since he took office.

Joe looked at his prime-ministerial notebook in front of him and contemplated drawing a cartoon of the leader of the opposition, but on second thoughts decided against it. You could never be sure who the person in charge of prime-ministerial sketchbooks was and whether they might be in any way inclined to pass on his efforts to some sort of newspaper.

'Are we sure they have WMDs?' Joe asked.

'Well, not exactly sure. At least they are not as sophisticated as ours.'

'I don't understand.'

'Well, they might actually not have any at all. But it's a start.'

'What's a start?'

'Well, the first step to having a WMD, is wanting one. Case proven!'

For Joe this didn't make much sense, but not much seemed to make sense around here. How could anyone argue like that without blushing?

'I am not going to start a war,' Joe said. 'A war is not on the agenda at this time,' he corrected himself, but wasn't sure what he meant any more.

'But, Prime Minister!' the foreign secretary said, 'I must insist that we take action now!'

'No!' Joe shouted and took a deep breath. The members of the cabinet looked at him flabbergasted.

'What is he doing?' the home secretary asked.

'He's holding his breath ... I'm begging you, Prime Minister, be reasonable.'

Joe wasn't sure how much longer he could hold his breath. Once he had fainted after one minute and eight seconds, but he was getting older.

'Very well, Prime Minister, as you wish.'

Relieved, Joe took a deep breath. 'As I said: a war is not on the agenda at this time.'

7

Even though his next appointment was only down the road, Joe was ushered into a limo. Before he had even thought about the possibility of facing traffic jams, sirens sounded from all directions and Joe's limo drove at high speed through the traffic, which quickly made room for him.

I'm beginning to like this, Joe thought, but immediately he felt guilty because deep in his heart he knew that he should have walked the few steps, prime minister or not. Charlie said he'd get used to it. In fact that was all she ever seemed to be saying. Joe was beginning to get used to that, too.

'You're having dinner with the Hungarian prime minister.'

'But I don't ...'

' ... eat meat.' Charlie interrupted. 'Yes, we know, but of course you would never say that in public.'

'I wouldn't?'

'The meat lobby would get angry.'

'But why?'

'Because the prime minister can't express any preferences.'

'I can't?'

'Unless it's British.'

'So I like ... '

'British beef, British eggs, British bacon ... '

'But if I had to ... '

'Eat?'

'Yes.'

'We're working on that.'

The limo stopped abruptly.

'What's happening?' Joe asked.

'A demonstration.'

'What are they demonstrating about?' Joe was curious.

'About the war.'

'What war?' Joe thought that if there was a war, he should be the first to know.

'They think there's going to be a war in the Middle East.'

'How did they get that idea?' Joe was genuinely surprised.

'Apparently you said that war is not on the agenda.'

Joe's heart sank. He should have known better. 'I'm going to explain it to them.'

'Good idea,' Charlie said. The limo started moving again. 'I'll set up an audience debate on *Newsfight* for you.'

Joe's heart sank. He knew all about these hand-picked audiences it was safe to debate with. Somehow they all sounded like Charlie when she was briefing him about what he may or may not be asked at prime minister's questions. 'No,' he said. 'I'd like to explain it *now*.'

'You mean ... ?'

'I'd like to get out of the car.'

'But you can't!' Charlie looked at him incredulously. 'You're the prime minister!'

'You're right, I *am* the prime minister and in my book that means that I can do pretty much what I like.'

'But it's not arranged ... it's ...' For the first time Charlie seemed lost for words. 'It's dangerous!'

'Stop!' Joe stared at Charlie, but the limo kept going.

Joe took a deep breath and Charlie raised her eyebrows. 'As you wish.' Charlie seemed to have the signal which made the driver stop the car, as if Joe's yelling wasn't clear enough.

The car stopped right next to the crowd, who seemed more startled than happily surprised. Joe pushed open the door and stepped outside. He was immediately surrounded by four bodyguards, who were so big that he felt that they might crush him any at moment. But being short and agile had its benefits and Joe slipped through their legs and escaped to the other side of the crowd.

'Here I am!' Joe announced to the demonstrators, who were still facing the wrong direction. 'It's me, Joe! Let me explain!'

But Joe immediately realised that Charlie had been right all along when an egg hit him on the forehead.

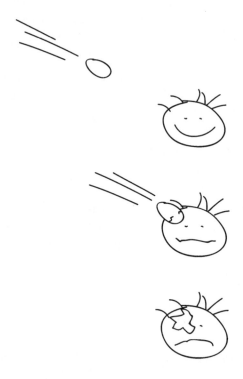

JOE REALISED THAT CHARLIE HAD BEEN RIGHT ALL
ALONG WHEN AN EGG HIT HIM ON THE FOREHEAD

8

The good thing about the egg was that Joe was allowed to go home early. As he closed the door to his flat in No 10, he realised that this was the first time he had had off since being elected.

He decided to run a bath as his hair felt all sticky. Whoever had been throwing the eggs was a pretty good shot, Joe thought as he climbed into the tub, and he supposed he could count himself lucky that the protester hadn't thrown anything more dangerous, like a pineapple.

As he was soaking in the tub, Joe realised that he was hungry and thought what a waste of perfectly good eggs it had been. And weren't protesters meant to throw *rotten* eggs? But Joe guessed rotten eggs where hard to come by, and it wouldn't make much sense to buy fresh ones and then delay protesting until they were rotten. That would take a lot of patience and he didn't think the protester was the patient type.

As his stomach rumbled, Joe started to get angry at the protester. After all, Joe had been elected, so it was pretty much up to him what he did as he had the trust of the electorate. Wasn't that how democracy was supposed to work? The losers would just have to put up with it until it was their turn.

After all over a third of those who had bothered

to vote had voted for him, but when Joe closed his eyes and imagined a cake sliced in half to represent how many people had voted, and then imagined that half cut into thirds, he was disappointed. That piece of cake would not be enough to feed anyone. He imagined the left-over piece, which looked much more inviting, and guessed that whoever would be in charge of the apathy party could change the world.

Joe was curious about why everyone hadn't voted in the election. Surely it must be because people were happy. Joe could count himself lucky to live in a country where people took so little interest in politics. After all, he believed, politics was for those who wanted to change things, not for those who were happy with what they already had.

Joe thought about what Charlie had done to his to-do list. She had handed Joe a thick bundle of papers. Charlie and her team had somehow managed to turn his nine-point list into a 235-page draft document. This was only a summary of a much longer one, Charlie had proudly said, which would follow sometime during the course of next parliament. Joe had scanned the document for the chocolate bit, but it was nowhere to be found.

After the soak in the tub, Joe was feeling very tired, but rather than get into bed he took out Charlie's document and flicked through it once more. There were so many words, but Joe struggled to find some substance. He took out the list, which was still in the back pocket of his trousers on his bathroom floor. As he unfolded it for what must have been the umpteenth time over the past six months, it was decidedly showing more wear and tear.

Joe had someone bring a sandwich and a hot chocolate, switched on the desk lamp in his study and carefully began to read through the document. Between the lines he could see that many of his ideas were still there, even though they had been reworded to make them more prime-ministerial. which he supposed was OK. To avoid any confusion, he amended his list accordingly:

Things to do when I rule the world:
1. Help the poor *help themselves*
2. ~~Steal from~~ *Tax* the rich *within reason (so they won't ~~imi~~ emigrate)*
3. No more wars *unless necessary*
4. Free chocolate for all *(but not so much your teeth fall out)*
5. All bullies ~~to be locked up~~ *to be given a stern warning (unless they work for me).*
6. ~~Ban all cars~~ *Increase ministerial salaries seven per cent above inflation*
7. ~~No more borders~~ Don't come here (unless you're rich)
8. ~~N~~Do more homework
9. ~~Always remember those less fortunate than yourself.~~ *Equal opportunities for all (done, sort of)*

Joe looked at the revised list and sighed. Is this what I went into politics for? But things take time,

Things to do when I rule the world:

1. Help the poor ~~help themselves~~.

2. ~~Steal from~~ **Tax** the rich (see 1) *within reason*
   (~~so they won't~~ *emit* ~~emigrate~~).

3. No more wars *unless necessary*

4. Free chocolate for all (*but not so much your teeth fall out*)

5. All bullies ~~to be locked up~~ *to be given a stern warning* (*unless they work for me*).

6. ~~Ban all cars~~ *Increase ministerial salaries seven per cent above inflation.*

7. ~~No more borders~~ *Don't come here (unless your rich)*

8. ~~No~~ more homework

9. ~~Always remember those less fortunate than yourself~~ *equal opportunities for all* (*Done, sort of*).

TO AVOID ANY CONFUSION,
JOE AMENDED HIS LIST

and he *had* time. He was young. He wished people were more patient and appreciated how difficult a job it really was to be prime minister. Joe had his five-year plan and he'd get back to the original list given time. And if that didn't work out, there'd be another five years.

But Joe couldn't help thinking about the protester. Why had he thrown the egg? Charlie had told Joe that they were protesting about a war he never would start, but Charlie had also told him that the opinion polls didn't look too good.

But why shouldn't people just press a button and decide on policy? That would mean there would be no need for politicians, but Joe guessed that people often weren't very good at making decisions and if people like the protester were in charge, things would soon turn out worse. Just like when he was hungry for fast food, he'd sometimes buy some, only to regret it almost as soon as he had finished it. Maybe Joe was like the chef of a restaurant whose job it was to make sure that the public only ordered what was good for them.

But whatever he tried to tell himself, Joe couldn't cheer himself up. Just when he had decided to call it a night, the phone rang. Joe picked it up, but just got a dial tone. It was the red one that was ringing.

9

'Hello?' Joe said.

'What do you want?' the voice at the other end snapped.

'*You* called *me*.'

'No, I didn't.' The man on other end of the line sounded rather irritated. 'You'd think I'd know if I called someone, wouldn't you?' Joe couldn't really even begin to answer that question, as he had no idea who he was taking to.

Joe decided to put his cards on the table. 'This is the prime minister.'

'Prime minister of what?' came the answer, rather rudely.

'Well, Great Britain. Well, Great Britain and Northern Ireland if you want to be picky.' And Joe thought the person on the other end did sound rather picky. He guessed he should have mentioned Gibraltar and the Falklands as well, but no one else ever did.

'Ah, the kid!'

Joe thought he could hear a snigger at the other end, but it might have been his imagination. He thought better not to mention it. 'Anyway,' Joe said. 'There I was minding my own business, I mean other people's business, when the phone rang, the red phone, and I picked it up. And here we are, having this rather useless conversation.'

'The red phone? Well, I guess then it must be important. What can I do for you?'

'I still think it was you who ca ...'

'Get on with it, sonny. Time is money. I'm busy!'

Busy doing what? Joe wondered. Busy calling people up who didn't want to be called up, he guessed. 'I suppose I could use some help!'

'Hah!'

'What is that supposed to mean?'

'I knew it! Out with it!'

Joe was thinking about the protester, Charlie and his cabinet, who all seem to be against him. 'I just want to help people and they don't seem at all ... grateful.'

Joe could make out a deep sigh at the other end, and somehow thought the person on the other end of the line understood.

'Tell me about it. If people get fed up with you, you gotta cheer them up.'

'With what?'

'Gotta distract their attention. Make them feel good about themselves.'

'But how?'

'We've been working on a few ideas. Could help you out there. It's a win-win situation.'

This all sounded good to Joe. 'What can I do?'

'Stand next to me, shoulder to shoulder,' the voice said.

'But I don't even know who you are.'

'I meant metaphysically speaking,' the voice said, but Joe was sure that it should have been metaphorical. 'You're either with us or against us.'

Joe could tell he was talking with a real politician now, one who knew the phrases. But still ... 'We don't really like wars here too much.' Joe said. 'Been there, done that.'

'Coulda fooled me!' the man on the other end laughed. 'Look I could use some help here, too.' The line was quiet. 'So, are you?'

'What?'

'With us or against us?'

'But ...'

'There is this country. I believe they have oil and WMDs.'

'How do you know?'

'I don't question it.'

'But ...'

'Lots of people don't want to do the right thing. Lots of paperwork stopping us from liberating them.'

'You mean the law?'

'Did what's his name, Churchill, need a piece of paper to go after the Krauts?'

Joe believed that he did, but the man on the other side didn't really sound like he could be argued with. 'I don't think I ...'

'Three, two, one ...'

It had gone ominously quiet on the other end of the line. Surely it couldn't be...? What a tricky devil, Joe thought.

'Are you holding your breath?' Joe asked suspiciously.

A muffled sound came from the other end.

'You know,' Joe said, 'I'm pretty good at holding

my breath, too. In fact, I held the world record for my class for several months.' Joe was worried that there was nothing coming from the other end of the line, but the transatlantic static noise confirmed that there was still a connection. Joe glanced up at his world clock. Over a minute had passed.

'Are you still there?' Joe asked and suddenly heard a loud thud from the other end. 'Are you all right?' he shouted down the line. 'Please say something!' Joe didn't know what to do. 'All right, all right I'll do whatever you say!'

'Thank you,' came the voice from the other end, suspiciously quickly, but a little out of breath. 'You'll hear from us post haste.'

Before Joe could say anything, the line went dead.

10

'Well, Prime Minister, there is some good news, some bad news and some not so bad news. What do you want to hear first?' The foreign secretary had woken Joe at 5am, and Joe had actually been grateful as he had slept very badly.

'The bad news,' Joe said.

'It doesn't work this way.'

'OK, the not so bad news.'

'Can I start with the good news?'

'OK.'

'Well, the good news is that the war is over.'

'Already?'

'It took precisely 24 minutes.'

Joe was relieved. That means that there couldn't have been many casualties. 'Did anyone get killed?'

'Er, two.'

Two people didn't sound too bad to Joe, but he guessed that was still two too many. 'Either of the two British?'

'Er, I meant two per cent of the population, Prime Minister.'

'And that's the good news?' A shiver went down Joe's spine. 'What's the bad news?'

'Well, there was what we call an intelligence failing.' If he had been in a better mood, Joe would have laughed. Where he came from, an 'intelligence failing' was simply called being stupid.

'What we took as an intercepted message about the location of weapons of mass destruction, actually got a tad scrambled. We found masses of destructed weapons, which oddly enough, is exactly what we asked them to do after the last war. Devious buggers. They tried to confuse us by doing exactly what we asked them to do.'

Joe sighed. How could he have been so careless not to have people double check the source of his intelligence before starting a war? And everyone had been so convincing. But he knew that if you wanted something to be true and wished for it hard enough, you could convince yourself of anything.

'And the not so bad news?' Joe asked wearily, but he didn't seem too hopeful.

'Well, we've discovered another country which also has masses of destructed weapons, which is only next door, so we wouldn't have to go far.'

'Go far to do what?' Joe knew what the foreign secretary was playing at, but didn't want to be the one to say it first.

'The similarities don't end there. It also has a foreigner in charge.' The foreign secretary sounded genuinely pleased at having found this coincidence. 'How about we invade that?'

Joe couldn't believe what he was hearing. 'And make another mistake?'

'If we make one mistake it looks careless, but if we make lots of mistakes, it may seem as if it's all part of a plan.'

To be fair, Joe was the first who would have to admit that this made sense. It reminded him how

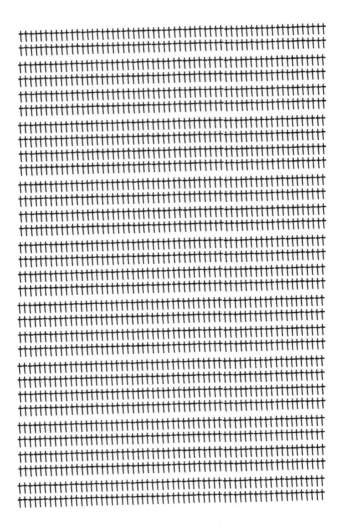

'DID ANYONE GET KILLED?' JOE ASKED.
'ER, TWO PER CENT OF THE POPULATION'

he once broke his gran's favourite picture frame and broke the other ones as well so he could blame it on a gust of wind. The only problem was that he had forgotten to open the window.

'If you're worried about the costs ... ' the foreign secretary said, 'they have oil as well, so the war will pay for itself.' The financial costs of going into a war had never worried Joe. Just like the cost of healthcare, doing the right thing should never have a price tag, but he guessed it was good to know.

'What are the alternatives?'

'They are not so good.'

'Tell me.'

'We ... er, you could say you made a terrible mistake.' That didn't sound too bad to Joe. After all, it was true. 'Of course you'd have to resign immediately.'

Joe's heart sank. He still had so many things to do. The back benches didn't look much fun, looking at everyone's dandruff and the opposition yelling at you without being able to answer back. And he was only a tenth of the way through his list of nine items, and even that wasn't going very well. He did need more time if he wanted to do good things for people. But no, this was simply wrong. 'I can't do it,' Joe said. 'I can't lie.'

'Who said anything about lying?'

'What do you mean?'

'You need to see the doctor.'

'But I'm not sick.'

11

One thing about working from home is that people can spring meetings on you while you are still wearing your pyjamas, but either the man waiting in Joe's front room was too polite or too unobservant to say anything.

'I hear you are having a problem,' the man got up as soon as Joe had entered the room.

'You can say that again.' Joe looked at the man suspiciously. 'Don't I know you?' Joe knew his face from somewhere, but couldn't quite place it.

'I'm your spin doctor.'

'What is a spin doctor?' He hadn't heard that phrase in his dictionary and decided to ask straight away, because it could be even more embarrassing to ask later.

The spin doctor sighed, seemingly disappointed at Joe's ignorance. 'Do you honestly think you've never required the services of a spin doctor?'

'Not as far as I know.' But Joe now remembered where he had seen him before. He usually arrived immediately after he had given interviews, at least he did at the beginning of Joe's career, when he hadn't quite mastered Charlie's vocabulary list.

'Let me explain,' the spin doctor looked down, as if he were studying the pattern of the carpet. 'It is a sad but nevertheless well-documented fact that the general public are not particularly bright. And journalists, who generally are a little brighter, compensate for it with laziness. But this works to our advantage.'

'You're losing me.' Truth be told, Joe's head had started to spin, so maybe the doctor was already at work. 'How?'

'They allow themselves to be spun. In fact, they are usually rather grateful that someone tells them what to report and how to report it.'

'You mean you teach them?' Joe asked, but somehow the spin doctor didn't strike him as the teaching type.

'Not exactly. It's more than imparting a way of thinking. Often people have no opinion, so you have to give it to them, and what better place to start than with language?'

Suddenly something dawned on Joe. 'You wrote the dictionary Charlie gave me?' That explained why 'spin doctor' wasn't included in it!

'You're learning fast.' The spin doctor looked up at him. 'So, how can I help?'

'I misled the British people.'

'Hold your horses! Careful what you say.'

'I started this war, and now I think that it may have been the wrong thing to do.'

'Why?'

'I've seen intelligence reports, which I should have realised were a little unreliable.'

'But you believed they were true?'

'Yes, I did.'

'But now you know that they were not?'

'Yes.' Joe realised that his partner in crime on

the other end of the phone also said 'believed' and never 'knew'.

'And?'

'I'm afraid I lied.'

'Was the lie in the interest of national security?'

'No,' Joe admitted. More in the interest of national insecurity, Joe reckoned, at least in hindsight.

'But it wasn't a lie at the time?'

'What do you mean?'

'Did you know that you were not telling the truth at the time?'

'No, of course not.'

'So where is your problem?'

'It was my job to make sure what I was saying was true. I am the prime minister. Who else could they depend on?'

'But what you told them was true.'

'No, it wasn't.'

'But you didn't know that at the time.'

'A thing is either true or false, isn't it?'

'It depends.'

'Depends on what?'

'There are always two aspects to a lie: the person telling it and the person believing it.'

'I don't get it.'

'It depends on what people want to hear.' Joe was confused. 'Are you to blame for telling people what they want to hear? Even if that includes you?'

'So I didn't lie?' Joe could feel a weight lifting from his shoulders.

'Not technically, no. Leave it with me.'

12

When Charlie brought in the newspapers the next morning, Joe could see that the spin doctor had done an excellent job turning disaster into triumph. Joe had managed almost single-handedly to bring down an evil dictator, whose human rights abuses had been bothering the civilised free world for ever.

No, oil didn't even come into it, Joe read himself to have said. *It was a matter of principle, and the whole country was behind me. Even Northern Ireland and ...* Joe was surprised to hear ... *Gibraltar.*

The spin doctor had hastily assembled a consortium of like-minded countries, now called the 'coalition of the willing'. Coincidentally, these were also the world's largest users of oil, along with a handful of countries who wanted to be the world's largest users of oil.

Joe dipped into his breakfast, relieved. As he put a soldier into his egg, he thought back to the protester. See! If you had only given me time, you'd have seen that I had a plan, even though, to be honest, it was also news to Joe that he did. All he had wanted was to do good for his country, and now here he was, improving the whole world.

Joe felt in his back pocket for his list, and looked at the points he had drawn up. How naive he had been back then, to think things were that simple.

Steal from the rich to give to the poor. The rich would have just moved away. No more cars, but where would that leave the workers? No more wars? Well, this one was in a good cause: to prevent a war which people had been fairly confident would happen sooner or later. Probably later, but it was better to be safe than sorry. As for free chocolate for all, invading Switzerland could not be entirely ruled out.

Joe sighed. Despite his good mood he couldn't help noticing that he hadn't achieved a single item on his list. But surely priorities change? As he finished his breakfast, he picked up the phone. He might have the country's – or at least the media's – approval, but there was one person whose opinion he was really curious about.

'Yes, Prime Minister?' Charlie's voice came immediately.

'Do you remember that man who threw the perfectly good egg?' Joe asked.

'Of course.'

'I'd like to speak to him.'

'Why?'

Joe knew it would be better not to tell Charlie the truth. 'I'd like to tell him off.'

'Excellent idea, but that has already been taken care of.'

'I just want to make sure that he understands.'

'I'm sure he does.'

'Do we know where he lives?' Joe insisted.

'Of course ...'

'Where?' When there was no reply, Joe thought

that the line had gone dead.

'He is prison.'

'In prison? For throwing an egg?'

'Not just that.'

'What else has he done?'

'He may throw other things.'

'And he was charged for that?'

'No, not exactly charged. We believe he's a terrorist ...'

'What about human rights?'

'I'm all in favour of human rights, but ...'

'So he hasn't had a trial?'

'But, Prime Minister, if there is a trial, there is a genuine risk that he may be freed.'

'I see,' Joe said. 'But I insist ...'

'It's too dangerous, Prime Minister.' Joe remembered that Charlie told him that it was too dangerous to get out of the car and that she'd been right.

'Maybe you're right,' Joe conceded.

'I'm glad you agree, Prime Minister,' Charlie said. 'We're doing so well in the polls today, it would be far too dangerous if the media got wind of you making a visit to Brixton prison.'

13

When the door to the visitor's room was opened
for him, Joe found that the egg thrower was much
shorter than he had imagined.

'I heard you were coming,' the protester said,
and Joe could see that there was a TV in the room,
showing silent news. A huge crowd could be seen
gathering outside the prison. Joe would have never
thought that his trip would get so much attention,
but he must have been the first prime minister to
walk out of Downing Street and ask for directions
to the bus stop for Brixton. A kind passenger even
gave him the change to pay for his trip, as he
hadn't seen any need to carry cash since he was in
office.

'Why are you here?' the protester asked and got
up as far as his restraints allowed, though he was
quickly forced to sit down again.

'Why did you throw it?'

'I didn't mean to. Really I didn't.'

'That's OK,' Joe said, and he wanted to tell him
that it was a waste of a perfectly good egg, but the
protester didn't need to be told off any more. In
fact, Joe thought he needed cheering up.

'It seemed like fun,' the protester said.

'What do you mean?'

'There were all these people standing around,
looking angry, and shouting. And everyone got

really excited when this car stopped and then this kid – you – appeared. And I'd just been shopping and I just … I just threw the egg … no reason really.'

'So you're not angry with me?'

'Angry? No. I didn't even know who you were until everyone jumped on me and dragged me to the police station and started interrogating me.'

Joe didn't know whether to laugh or to cry. 'Did you vote?'

'Vote?'

'At the last election?'

'Why bother?'

'Aren't you angry?'

'Why?'

'Well, you're imprisoned here for starters, without trial, for no reason.'

'I suppose. But what's that got to do with anything?'

'Well, you could start by voting out of office the people who keep you here.'

'You're in charge?'

'Not me, but my home secretary.' And Charlie and the cabinet for passing stupid laws and me for allowing this to happen, Joe thought, but he decided that it was better not share this.

'But the other parties all sound just as bad. They never talk about anything. They just say what they think we want to hear.'

'Everyone?'

'Well, the ones that have a chance.'

'If everyone voted for what they believed in, things would be a lot different around here,' Joe said. 'Now, if you excuse me, I've got a bus to catch.' Joe turned to leave.

'Are you going to let me go?' the protester said.

'Yes.'

'Can you do that?'

'Sure.' Joe didn't feel much like holding his breath, but he'd be happy to do it for a good cause. Joe had heard enough. He turned to leave.

'Sorry about the egg,' the protester said. 'I know it was a perfectly good one. I know protesters are supposed to throw rotten ones, but I wouldn't know where to get one anyway. Maybe there's a gap in the market.'

14

Joe looked at the motley crew that had assembled in his office. The home secretary, the foreign secretary and the rest of the cabinet had come to hear what Joe had to say.

Joe looked at Charlie. Even she seemed curious, for the first time unsure of what was to come. Joe thought it suited her.

'Drastic times require drastic measures,' Joe said and Charlie looked pleased to see that Joe had learnt his vocabulary. 'And I've been especially interested in what the focus groups have been saying.'

The home secretary looked at Joe curiously.

'There is an election coming up and immigration always comes out as the top concern of the man in the street.' Well, whatever men in the street Charlie and his friends assembled for the focus groups.

'We can't afford to alienate the voters. It's time to sort out this immigration problem once and for all.'

The home secretary continued to look curious as Joe continued. 'We're going to have no more immigration and no more immigrants! In fact we won't have any foreigners at all!' Joe stood up triumphantly. 'We're going to get rid of them all!'

'I beg your pardon?' The home secretary looked as if he thought Joe had gone mad, but Joe knew that he had tapped into something that appealed to him.

'We'll get rid of all foreigners at a stroke!'

'We'd never get away with it!' The home secretary stood up and beamed. 'But the man in the street would applaud you, surely. And just think of all the money we'd save. No more printing leaflets in a thousand incomprehensible languages ... Finally someone says what's been on my mind all along!'

'That's the spirit!' Joe said. 'Was that so hard?'

'I don't understand.'

Joe quietened him with a glance. 'I meant we are going to open our borders to everyone who wants to come here. Everyone who wants one can have a British passport. No more borders, no more immigration officials, no more passports ...' Joe said quietly, but this time he knew that everyone was listening. 'What did *you* mean?'

'What?' the home secretary seemed flustered. 'I thought you meant ... '

'I know what you meant,' Joe said.

'I didn't mean to ... '

'No more foreigners, and just think of it,' Joe said, 'no more home secretary!' Joe wished he had a hidden lever to pull so a trap door under the home secretary would open and dispatch him straight to Henley-on-Thames, but no such luck. He should look into that.

'It's impossible!' the home secretary said, and Joe was sure that he briefly contemplated holding his breath, but, quickly changed his mind. 'But ... '

Charlie turned to Joe, disappointed. 'Do you really want to be remembered as the prime minister who opened the floodgates to immigration? We were doing fine. A reform here and there, maybe another term, and when you've finished you have your whole life in front of you. You can even finish school.'

'You didn't understand. Am I going to open the borders and open the floodgates to immigration? I don't know, but I'm certainly going to talk about it.' Joe looked around the table.

'So here are my wishes: all of you say what's on your mind. And if I don't see one major gaffe reported in every paper and on every news programme about every single one of you first thing tomorrow, I am going to find someone who can be more disagreeable. Only an onslaught of errors, disagreements and gaffes is going to convince the people that we are serious about discussion.' Joe took a deep breath.

'I want public debate about everything. Should we abolish borders to make the world fairer for everyone? I don't know. Should we ban cars, to reclaim the streets for our pensioners and our children? I don't know. Should we invade Switzerland for the chocolate? I am leaning towards it. And for God's sake, somebody prepare a calculation to work out how many deaths of ordinary people can be reasonably justified per barrel of oil.' Joe stood up. 'Now, if you'll excuse me, I have to apologise to the nation.'

'Apologise for what?' Charlie seemed

flabbergasted.

'For having turned into a politician.' Joe opened the door. 'And then I'm going to call an election to see whether they still want me.'

15

It turned out that the voters didn't want him. Well,
that's not entirely true: some did vote for Joe, but
just as many voted for the Greens, some for the
left, some for the right, some for the middle and
some for the left-of-centre. The right-of-centre
didn't do so well, though, but the left-of-the-
middle-of-centre more than made up for it. The
resulting government provided some of the liveliest
discussions the country had ever seen and
parliament's TV ratings were only second to the
annual *Politician's Big Brother*.

But parliament did adopt some of Joe's
suggestions: spin doctors and their phrase books
were banned and from then on there was more
than one right answer to each question. Rhetorical
questions were outlawed in the House of
Commons and the Speaker of the house had a big
lever for a new trap-door device for any MP who
broke the new rules. Where the trap-door led was
anybody's guess, as none of the disgraced
politicians were ever heard of again. Whips were
retrained to spot any unusual agreement on
controversial subjects, and encouraged to chip in
with far-fetched and radical proposals of their own.

Complex issues were welcomed and any policies
which were immediately agreed by the majority of
MPs were immediately marked as highly suspicious

and passed on to a select committee.

All legislation which had lain buried for the past twenty years was resurrected and scrutinised afresh by a new committee headed by the protester and some of the new pals he had made during his incarceration – not all on the left and even some royalty. It was the most multicultural committee Britain had ever seen.

As for Joe, he didn't finish school as he was working far too hard to find a peaceful solution to the problem of making Switzerland hand over all of its chocolate.

Also from Pinter & Martin

Childbirth without Fear
Grantly Dick-Read
with a foreword by Michel Odent
paperback, £8.99, ISBN 0953096469

'When I was heavily pregnant with my first child 25 years ago, this book
fell into my hands. That was the start of my belief in natural childbirth,
which eventually led to four great births of my own and the founding of
my life's work in the Active Birth Movement. Grantly Dick-Read's
message is inspirational and even more relevant today than when this
book was first published. Every pregnant mother should read it.'
Janet Balaskas – Author of *New Active Birth*

Natural Childbirth
Grantly Dick-Read
audio CD, £9.99, 52min
An extraordinary documentary record of the birth
of a baby delivered by the author of *Childbirth without Fear*.

Thank you, Dr Lamaze
Marjorie Karmel
paperback, £8.99, ISBN 0953096483

Inspired by Grantly Dick-Read's *Childbirth without Fear*, Marjorie Karmel,
an American woman pregnant with her first child in Paris, consulted
with pioneering French obstetrician Dr Lamaze. This bestselling account
of her experiences of antenatal education and hospital care on both
sides of the Atlantic and the birth of her children would change for ever
the way many women give birth.

Obedience to Authority
Stanley Milgram
with a foreword by Jerome Bruner
paperback, £8.99, ISBN 0953096483

Volunteers are invited to a scientific laboratory under the pretence
of participating in a study about the effects of punishment on learning.
They are instructed by an experimenter to administer an electric shock
of increasing intensity to a 'learner' every time he makes a mistake.
How many, if any, would go right up the scale to 450 volts?
The implications of Stanley Milgram's extraordinary findings are
devastating. From the Holocaust to Vietnam's My Lai massacre, from
Bosnia to Iraq's Abu Ghraib prison, *Obedience to Authority* goes some way
towards explaining how ordinary people can commit the most horrific
of crimes if placed under the influence of a malevolent authority.

'A masterpiece'. NEW STATESMAN

'Milgram's work is of first importance, not only in explaining how it is
that men submit, but also in suggesting how better they may rebel.'
SUNDAY TIMES

'The resonance is deep, from Auschwitz to My Lai, the connections
unavoidable; the implications altogether cheerless.' ROLLING STONE

The Little Driver
Martin Wagner
paperback, £5, ISBN 0953096459

'A delightful fairy tale...highly recommended for children and adults alike. *The Little Driver* will make you laugh, dream and perhaps think a little differently about the world around us.'
Lucie Lebrova – CARBUSTER

'Billed as "an anti-car book for a new generation", *The Little Driver* is a gem, easily negotiating the many dead ends encountered when questioning car culture. Like many eight-year-old boys, Joe is obsessed with cars, but when his wish suddenly comes true he embarks on a journey he wasn't expecting. Full of wit and dry observation, much of the beauty of *The Little Driver* is in the way it captures the visceral thrill and smug pride Joe feels when first behind the wheel of his shiny red sports car, and then peels away the layers as Joe's encounters with selfish drivers, traffic jams, pollution and road-building slowly force him to question his love of the automobile.' Andrew Brackenbury – ERGO

Pinter & Martin publications are available from all good bookshops and direct from the publishers.

Send a cheque (free p&p) to:

Pinter & Martin Ltd, 6 Effra Parade, London SW2 1PS, Tel 020-7737 6868, info@pinterandmartin.com

or order on line **www.pinterandmartin.com**